I
SAW
ESAU

The Publisher, the Artist, the Editors

I
SAW
ESAU

The Schoolchild's Pocket Book

EDITED BY

IONA AND PETER OPIE

ILLUSTRATED BY

MAURICE SENDAK

CANDLEWICK PRESS
CAMBRIDGE, MASSACHUSETTS

First U.S. edition 1992

This edition first published in
Great Britain in 1992 by
Walker Books Ltd., London.

Original edition first published by
Williams and Northgate Ltd.,
London, 1947, as
I Saw Esau: traditional rhymes of youth

ISBN 1-56402-046-0
ISBN 1-56402-072-X (limited edition)
Library of Congress Catalog Card
Number 91-71845
Library of Congress Cataloging-in-
Publication information is available.

10 9 8 7 6 5 4 3 2 1

Printed in Italy by L.E.G.O., Vicenza

Candlewick Press
2067 Massachusetts Avenue
Cambridge, Massachusetts 02140

To W. B.
for twenty-four
good reasons

Iona Opie

For James Marshall
friend and
colleague

◄━━━━━━━━━━━━━━━━►

Maurice Sendak

INTRODUCTION

In the autumn of 1946, Peter and I forswore the pleasures of London and retired to a cottage in Surrey. With us went the two-year-old James and a large accumulation of traditional rhymes. The following year Robert Opie was born, and *I Saw Esau: traditional rhymes of youth* was published.

Esau was the first book Peter and I produced together. It was a recognition of the particular genus of rhymes that belongs to schoolchildren. They were clearly not rhymes that a grandmother might sing to a grandchild on her knee. They have more oomph and zoom; they pack a punch. Many are directly concerned with the exigencies of school life: the need for a stinging reply when verbally attacked; the need for comic complaints in the face of persecution or the grinding drudgery of schoolwork; the need to know some clever rhymes by heart, with which to win popularity.

They pass from one child to another without adult interference.

The book came out in a small edition typical of those days of paper rationing. It brought us some lifelong friends and correspondents, and the *British Weekly* said, "We imagine the authors will be found to have 'started something.'" While we were going on with the "something" we had started, for the next thirty-five years, we almost forgot about *Esau.*

After Peter died, in 1982, and after two half-finished books had been finished, my life exploded into a series of amazing adventures. First of all there was the fundraising appeal to enable the Bodleian Library in Oxford to acquire the Opie Collection of Children's Literature, for which Sebastian Walker, founder of Walker Books, published *Tail Feathers from Mother Goose.* That was, for me, a discovery of line and color, and the whole world of illustration. Then came the sequels.

Sebastian said he could not do without his Opie "fix," and, with *Esau* in the cupboard, how could I deny him? He put the one remaining copy in his pocket (it measures seven and a half by five inches) and flew it across the Atlantic to show to Maurice Sendak. Maurice liked it, and there in the foyer of the Algonquin Hotel it was transferred to Maurice's pocket.

As the schoolchild riddle says, "The land was white, the seed was black": we had performed our act of faith, and we waited for the seed to grow. Something wonderful was bound to happen, for, as Marcus Aurelius said, "Nature delights in change, and in obedience to her all things are now done well." I looked at the rhymes again, and at the notes at the end of the book; forty years had elapsed since the first edition, and it was obvious that some rhymes had to go out and others come in. Amelia Edwards, art director at Walker Books, made a special copy of this new version for Maurice to carry around in his pocket wherever he went. He could scribble on the pages and fill in the spaces whenever he felt like it.

Now, with Sendak illustrations, the book has a new strength and an extra dimension. It is more than ever a declaration of a child's brave defiance in the face of daunting odds. A child *is* Jack the Giant Killer and Horatius defending the bridge; we rely on him to be so, as we rely on new growth in spring. So this is his pocket book, his *vade mecum* and armory (and those with a Jungian child still inside them may carry it in their pockets, too). He can see that even if Dr. Fell chops a boy's limbs off one by one, the severed head can get its own back, good-humoredly, with an audacious rhyme. His power, he learns, is so great that he can eat his own mother if need be (there she is, safely inside him, on page 74); but he knows that if he wants her to, she will turn herself into a tree to shelter him from the rain. In Maurice Sendak's pictures, the child always wins.

The best antidote to the anxieties and disasters of life is laughter; and this children seem to understand almost as soon as they are born. If laughter is lacking, they create it; if it is offered to them, they relish it. Here in this book is a feast of laughter. I recommend a first course at the Cramit Inn on page 42, followed by the sluglike baby crawling across pages 40 and 41, the supremely haughty child on page 34 (who is pretending imperviousness whilst being aware that words are the worst weapons of all), the pudding in "Up the Ladder and Down the Wall" (pages 68 and 69), which looks remarkably like a soggy baby, and the *W* figure in the Twentieth-Century Alphabet (page 104), who is doubling his fortune by stealing from posh-'n'-pompous France.

It is a help, this book, in our universal predicament. We find we are born, so we might as well stay and do as well as we can, and while we are here we can at least enjoy the endearing absurdities of humankind.

Iona Opie

Connie Onnie Naughty Tommy

Eating Nellie's Toffee Stick

BEGINNING OF TERM

1

Here we are, back again !
Lots of work and lots of pain.

"Esau"

And Other Dramas

2

I saw Esau kissing Kate,
The fact is we all three saw;
For I saw him,
And he saw me,
And she saw I saw Esau.

3

" I've got a lad and he's double double-jointed.
He gave me a kiss and made me disappointed.
He gave me another, to match the other – "
" My word, Marlene, I'll tell your mother ! "

4

Quick ! quick !
　　The cat's been sick.

Where ? where ?
　　Under the chair.

Hasten ! hasten !
　　Fetch the basin.

Alack ! alack !
　　It is too late,
The carpet's in
　　An awful state.

No ! no !
　　It's all in vain,
For she has licked it
　　Up again.

5

Oh dear me !
Mother caught a flea,
Put it in a tea pot
And made a cup of tea.
When she put the milk in
The flea came to the top;
When she put the sugar in
The flea went POP !

6

It's raining, it's pouring,
　　The old man's snoring.
He got into bed
　　And bumped his head
And couldn't get up in the morning.

7

A bug and a flea
　　Went out to sea
To fight the Spanish Armada.
The bug was drowned
　　And the flea was found
On the back of a dirty old sailor.

CHARACTERS

8

Queen, Queen, Caroline,
Washed her hair in turpentine;
Turpentine to make it shine,
Queen, Queen, Caroline.

9

There was a man who always wore
A saucepan on his head.
I asked him what he did it for –
" I don't know why, " he said.
" It always makes my ears so sore,
I am a foolish man.
I think I'll have to take it off,
And wear a frying pan. "

10

Thomas a Didymus, hard of belief,
Sold his wife for a pound of beef;
When the beef was eaten, good lack !
Thomas a Didymus wished her back.

11

Peter's Pop kept a lollipop shop,
And the lollipop shop kept Peter.

12

There were three ghostesses
Sitting on postesses
Eating buttered toastesses
And greasing their fistesses
Right up to their wristesses.
Weren't they beastesses
To make such feastesses !

13

I know a washerwoman, she knows me,
She invited me to tea.
Guess what we had for supper –
Stinking fish and bread and butter.

14

Patience is a virtue,
Virtue is a grace;
And Grace is a little girl
Who doesn't wash her face.

NONSENSE

15

One fine day in the middle of the night
Two dead men got up to fight.
A blind man came to see fair play,
A dumb man came to shout hurray.

16

I was in the garden
A-picking of the peas.
I busted out a-laughing
To hear the chickens sneeze.

17

One bright September morning in
    the middle of July,
The sun lay thick upon the ground,
    the snow shone in the sky.
The flowers were singing gaily,
    the birds were full of bloom;
I went upstairs to the cellar
    to clean a downstairs room.
I saw ten thousand miles away
    a house just out of sight,
It stood alone between two more
    and it was black-washed white.

18

When I was a chicken
As big as a hen,
My mother hit me
And I hit her again;
My father came in,
And he ordered me out,
So I up with my fist
And I gave him a clout.

19

I asked my mother for fifty cents
To see the elephant jump the fence;
He jumped so high he reached the sky
And didn't come back till the Fourth of July.

20

Apples and oranges, four for a penny,
You're a good scholar to count so many.
E.O., down below,
Father and Mother and dirty Joe.
Joe went out to sell his eggs,
He met a man with painted legs,
Painted legs and crooked toes,
That's the way the money goes.

INSULTS

21

Tommy Johnson is no good,
Chop him up for firewood;
When he's dead, boil his head,
Make it into gingerbread.

22

Donkey walks on four legs
    And I walk on two;
The last one I saw
    Was very like you.

23

You limb of a spider,
    You leg of a toad,
You little black devil,
    Get out of my road.

24

Tell her ! smell her !
Kick her down the cellar.

RETALIATION

25

Sticks and stones
May break my bones,
But words will never hurt me.

[*Reply to those calling one names*]

26

What! What!
Go to pot!
Cats' tails all hot,
You're an ass and I'm not.

[Reply to one continually saying "What?"]

27

Different people have different 'pinions;
Some like apples and some like inions.

[Reply to one who disagrees]

28

Any silly little soul
Easily can pick a hole.

[*Reply to a fault-finder*]

29

Sit on your thumb
Till more room do come.

[*Reply to "Where shall I sit?"*]

REALITY

30

All the girls in our town live a happy life,
    Except J.C. –
She wants a husband, a husband she shall have,
A dicky, dicky dandy, a daughter of her own.
Send her upstairs, put her to bed,
Send for the doctor before she is dead.
In comes the doctor, out goes the cat,
In comes Jimmie with his chimney hat.
I'm saucy, Jimmie says, I need a bonnie lassie.
    The rose is red,
    The violet's blue,
    Sugar is sweet,
    And so are you.
    If I stay
    Mother will say
    I'm playing with the boys
    Up the way.

31

House to let, enquire within,
Men turned out for drinking gin,
Smoking tobacco and pinching snuff.
Don't you think that's quite enough ?

32

Lay the cloth, knife and fork,
Bring me up a leg of pork.
If it's lean, bring it in,
If it's fat, take it back,
Tell the old woman I don't want that.

33

Mother made a seedy cake –
Gave us all the bellyache.

34

Cease your chatter
And mind your platter.

35

It rains, it pains,
It patters, it docks,
It makes little ladies
Take up their white frocks.
The rain is done,
The wind is down;
Put on your best,
And go to town.

36

Vote, vote, vote for (Billy Martin),
    Chuck old (Ernie) out the door –
If it wasn't for the law
    I would punch him on the jaw,
And we don't want (Ernie) anymore.

[*Election song*]

GRACES

37

Bless the meat,
Damn the skin.
Open your mouth
And cram it in.

38

Lord be praised, my belly's raised
An inch above the table;
And I'll be blowed if I've not stowed
As much as I am able.

RIDDLES

39

It is in the rock, but not in the stone;
It is in the marrow, but not in the bone;
It is in the bolster, but not in the bed;
It is not in the living, nor yet in the dead.

40

As I was going over London Bridge
    I met with a Westminster scholar.
He pulled off his cap an' drew off his glove,
    And wished me a very good morrow.
What was his name ?

41

    The land was white,
       The seed was black;
    It'll take a good scholar
       To riddle me that.

42

Brothers and sisters have I none,
But that man's father is my father's son.

MORE CHARACTERS

43

Eaper Weaper, chimney sweeper,
Had a wife and couldn't keep her.
Had another, didn't love her –
Up the chimney he did shove her.

44

Truth, Truth, nobody's daughter,
   Took off her clothes
      And jumped into the water.

45

Moses supposes his toeses are roses,
But Moses supposes erroneously.
For Moses he knowses his toeses aren't roses,
As Moses supposes his toeses to be.

46

Piggy on the railway, picking up stones,
Up came an engine and broke Piggy's bones.
" Oh ! " said Piggy, " that's not fair. "
" Oh ! " said the driver, " I don't care. "

47

Nellie Bligh caught a fly
Going home from school,
Put it in a hot mince pie
Waiting by to cool.

48

Sam, Sam, dirty old man,
Washed his face in a frying pan,
Combed his hair with a leg of a chair,
Sam, Sam, dirty old man.

SCHOOL LAW

49

My finger's wet,
   My finger's dry,
God strike me dead
   If I tell a lie.
Touch my heart,
   Touch my knee,
This shall forever
   A secret be.

[*Binding oath*]

50

Hangy Bangy cut my throat
At ten o'clock at night;
Hang me up, hang me down,
Hang me all about the town.

[*Another oath*]

51

A nip for new,
Two for blue,
Sixteen
For bottle green.

[*Punishment for wearing new clothes*]

52

Order in the gallery !
Silence in the pit !
The people in the boxes
Can't hear a bit.

[*Call for silence*]

53

I built my house, I built my walls,
I don't care where my chimney falls.

[*Warning cry, when throwing*
something up in the air]

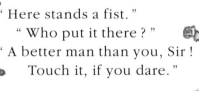

54

" Here stands a fist. "
" Who put it there ? "
" A better man than you, Sir !
Touch it, if you dare. "

[*Challenge to a fight*]

55

The moon shines bright
And the stars give a light.
We'll see to kiss a pretty lass
At ten o'clock at night.

[*Gang cry*]

56

It's time, I believe,
For us to get leave:
The little dog says
It isn't, it is, it isn't, it is…

[*To decide whether schooltime is over*]

NARRATIVES

57

The boy stood in the supper room
    Whence all but he had fled;
He'd eaten seven pots of jam
    And he was gorged with bread.

" Oh, one more crust before I bust ! "
    He cried in accents wild;
He licked the plates, he sucked the spoons –
    He was a vulgar child.

There came a hideous thunderclap –
    The boy – oh ! where was he ?
Ask of the maid who mopped him up,
    The bread crumbs and the tea.

58

I went downtown
To meet Mrs. Brown.
She gave me a nickel
To buy a pickle;
The pickle was sour,
I bought me a flower;
The flower was yellow,
I bought me a fellow;
The fellow was sick,
I gave him a kick,
And that is the end
Of my arithmetic.

59

Moses was a holy man,
Children he had seven,
He thought he'd hire a donkey cart
And drive them all to heaven.
On the road he lost his way,
He thought he knew it well,
He overturned the donkey cart
And landed them in — .

60

The rain it raineth all around
Upon the just and unjust fella;
But chiefly on the just because
The unjust stole the just's umbrella.

61

Hi-tiddley-i-ti, brown bread!
I saw a sausage fall down dead.
Up came a butcher with a great big knife,
Up jumped the sausage and ran for his life –
Hi-tiddley-i-ti, brown bread!

62

Oh the gray cat piddled in the white cat's eye,
The white cat said, " Cor blimey ! "
" I'm sorry, Sir, I piddled in your eye,
I didn't know you was behind me. "

63

Tom tied a kettle to the tail of a cat;
Jill put a stone in the blind man's hat;
Bob threw his grandmother down the stairs –
And they all grew up ugly and nobody cares.

Teasing and Repartee

64

" Have you got a sister ? "
" The beggarman kissed her ! "
" Have you got a brother ? "
" He's made of India rubber ! "
" Have you got a baby ? "
" It's made of bread and gravy ! "

65

I wouldn't be you
    For half a crown,
You kissed a lady
    And knocked her down.

[*To make a boy blush*]

66

" What's your name ? "
" Butter and tame.
  If you ask me again
  I'll tell you the same. "

67

Tit for tat,
Butter for fat,
If you kill my dog
I'll kill your cat.

68

I beg your pardon,
Grant your grace;
I hope the cows
Will spit in your face.

69

A cat may look at a king.
A man may look at his brother.
You may look at an ugly thing
And we all may look at each other.

[*To someone who doesn't like being stared at*]

Counting-out Rhymes

70

Hinx, minx, the old witch winks,
  The fat begins to fry.
Nobody at home but jumping Joan,
  Father, mother and I.
Stick, stock, stone dead,
  Blind man can't see;
Every knave will have a slave,
  You or I must be HE.

71

Eggs, butter, cheese, bread,
  Stick, stock, stone dead.
Stick him up, stick him down,
  Stick him in the old man's crown.

72

As Eenty Feenty Halligolun
The cat went out to get some fun.
He got some fun and tore his skin
As Eenty Feenty Halligolin.

73

Onery, twoery,
    Ziccary zan,
Hollow bone, crack-a-bone,
    Ninery, ten.
Spit, spot,
    It must be done.
Twiddlum, twaddlum,
    Twenty-one.

ONE

TWO

THREE

FOUR

FIVE

SIX

SEVEN

All good children go to heaven.
Penny on the water, tuppence on the sea,
Threepence on the railway, and out goes SHE.

GAME RHYMES

75

Up the ladder and down the wall,
Penny an hour will serve us all.
You buy butter and I'll buy flour,
And we'll have a pudding in half an hour.
     With –
        salt,
            mustard,
                vinegar,
                    pepper.

[*Skipping*]

76

Half a pint of porter,
    Penny on the can.
Hop there and back again
    If you can.

[*Hopping*]

77

Mother, Mother, I am ill!
Send for the doctor! Yes, I will.
Doctor, Doctor, shall I die?
Yes, my child, and so shall I.
When I die pray tell to me,
How many coaches will there be?
One, two, three, four...

All: Then we're respectable.

[*Skipping*]

78

Cold meat, mutton pies,
Tell me when your mother dies.
I'll be there to bury her –
Cold meat, mutton pies.

[*Skipping*]

79

Not last night but the night before,
Twenty-four robbers
Came knocking at the door.
As I ran out to let them in
This is what they said to me:

Spanish lady turn right round,
Spanish lady touch the ground,
Spanish lady do the high kicks,
Spanish lady do the splits.

[*Skipping*]

80

Black currant, red currant, raspberry tart,
Tell me the name of your sweetheart.
A, B, C, D ...

[*Skipping*]

81

I went to my father's garden,
And found an Irish farthing.
I gave it to my mother
To buy a baby brother.
My brother was so nasty,
I baked him in a pasty,
The pasty wasn't tasty
So I threw it over the garden wall,
I threw it over the garden wall.
   Die once !
      Die twice !
Die three times and never no more,
And never – no – more !

[*Swinging*]

82

Mademoiselle
She went to the well,
She didn't forget
Her soap and towel.
She washed her hands,
She wiped them dry,
She said her prayers,
She jumped up high.

[*Ball against wall*]

83

Tid, mid, misere,
Carling, palm, paste-egg day.
Sister Sarah died in sin;
Dig a hole and put her in.
Dig it deep and dig it narrow,
Dig it like a wheel barrow.
Set a cup upon a rock,
Mark me one-O-pot.

[*Hopscotch*]

84

Matthew, Mark, Luke and John,
Hold the horse till I leap on;
When I leapt on I could not ride,
I fell off and broke my side.

[*Riding piggy back*]

GUILE — MALICIOUS

85

I one my mother.
  I two my mother.
I three my mother.
  I four my mother.
I five my mother.
  I six my mother.
I seven my mother.
  I ate my mother.

86

Adam and Eve and Pinch-me
Went down to the river to bathe;
Adam and Eve were drowned,
Who d'you think was saved ?

87

I went up one pair of stairs.
  Just like me.
I went up two pairs of stairs.
  Just like me.
I looked out of the window.
  Just like me.
And there I saw a monkey.
  Just like me.

88

I'll go to A.
  I'll go to B.
I'll go to C.
  I'll go to D.
I'll go to E.
  I'll go to F.
I'll go to G.
  I'll go to H.
I'll go to I.
  I'll go to J.
I'll go to K.
  I'll go to L.

GUILE – INNOCENT

89

Charles the First walked and talked
Half an hour after his head was cut off.

[*Punctuation is important!*]

90

Every lady in the land
Has twenty nails upon each hand
Five and twenty on hands and feet;
All this is true without deceit.

[*More punctuation*]

91

Infir taris,
Inoak noneis.
Inmud eelsare,
Inclay noneare.
Mareseat oats,
Goatseativy.

MORE INSULTS

92

He that loves Glass without G
Take away L and that is he.

93

Robinson one,
Robinson two,
Biggest monkeys in the zoo.

94

Red, white, and blue,
I don't speak to you.

95

Birds of a feather flock together,
And so do pigs and swine;
Rats and mice will have their choice,
And so will I have mine.

Still More
Characters

96

Charlie, Charlie, in the tub,
Charlie, Charlie, pulled out the plug.
Oh my goodness, oh my soul,
There goes Charlie down the hole.

97

Caroline Pink, she fell down the sink,
She caught the Scarlet Fever,
Her husband had to leave her.
She called in Doctor Blue
And he caught it too –
Caroline Pink from China Town.

98

Nebuchadnezzar the King of the Jews
Sold his wife for a pair of shoes;
When the shoes began to wear
Nebuchadnezzar began to swear;
When the shoes got worse and worse
Nebuchadnezzar began to curse;
When the shoes were quite worn out
Nebuchadnezzar began to shout.

99

Annie ate jam,
Annie ate jelly.
Annie went to bed
With a pain in her belly.

100

Who are you? A dirty old man.
I've always been so since the day I began.
Mother and Father were dirty before me,
Hot and cold water has never come o'er me.

101

Mary Pary Pinder
Peeped through the winder;
Mother come
And smacked her bum
And cut her little finger.

VERBAL FUN

102

I scream,
    You scream,
  We all scream
    For ice-cream.

103

I slit a sheet,
  A sheet I slit,
A new beslitten sheet was it.

[*A trick tongue twister*]

104

Pease-porridge hot, pease-porridge cold,
Pease-porridge in the pot – nine days old.
Spell me that in four letters.

105

To a semicircle add a circle,
The same again repeat,
Add to these a triangle
And then you'll have a treat.

106

" What's your name ? "
" Mary Jane. "
" Where do you live ? "
" Womber Lane. "
" What do you do ? "
" Keep a school. "
" How many scholars ? "
" Twenty-two. "
" How many more ? "
" Twenty-four. "
" What's your number ? "
" Cucumber. "

[*Quick-fire dialogue*]

107

Railroad Crossing – Look out for the cars !
  Can you spell that without any "R"s ?

108

How much wood could a woodchuck chuck
If a woodchuck could chuck wood ?
As much wood as a woodchuck could chuck,
If a woodchuck could chuck wood.

[*A tongue twister*]

BOOK PROTECTION

109

Steal not this book for fear of shame,
For in it is the owner's name;
And if this book you chance to borrow,
Return it promptly on the morrow.
Or when you die the Lord will say,
Where's that book you stole away?
And if you say you do not know,
The Lord will answer, Go below!

110

If this book should chance to roam –
Box its ears and send it home.

111

Do not steal this book, my lad,
    For lots of money it cost my dad;
And if he finds you, he will say,
    " Go to Boston jail today! "

112

This book is one thing,
My fist is another;
Steal not the one
For fear of the other.

113

Who folds a leaf down,
The devil toast brown;
Who makes mark or blot,
The devil toast hot;
Who steals this book
The devil shall cook.

Book Desecration

114

If any man should see this book
He should at note 114 look.

115

If my name you wish to see
Look on page one-five-three.

116

By hook or by crook
I'll be last in this book.

117

By pen or by paint
I'll see that you ain't.

118

By the aid of my quill
I'll be hanged if you will.

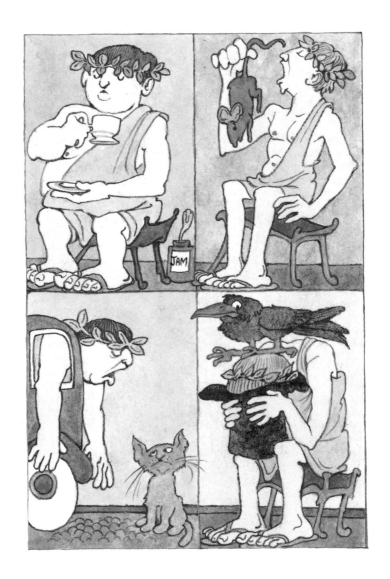

MOCK SCHOLASTIC

LOONY LATIN

119

Brutus adsum jam forte,
   Caesar aderat.
Brutus sic in omnibus,
   Caesar sic inat.

120

Is ab ile heres ergo,
   Fortibus es in ero.
Nobile themis trux,
   Se vatacinum – pes an dux.

121–123

VARIATIONS ON A THEME

Amo, amas,
    I had a little lass;
Amas, amat,
    And it grew very fat;
Amat, amamus,
    It grew very famous;
Amamus, amatis,
    I fed it on potatoes;
Amatis, amant,
    But it died of want.

Amo, amas,
I loved a lass, and she was tall and slender.
Sweet cowslip's grace,
Her nominative case,
And she's of the feminine gender.
Horum scorum, sunt divorum,
Harum scarum dyvo,
Sing song merry diggle, periwig and hat band,
Hic, haec, horum, genitivo.

Amo, amas,
    I love a lass;
Amamus, amatis,
    How sad her fate is.

124

Ego sum,
　　　I am,
Parvus homo,
　　　a little man,
Aptus ludere,
　　　ready to play,
Totam diem,
　　　all the day,
In gramine,
　　　on the grass,
Cum puella,
　　　with a lass.

125

Sum –
I am a gentleman;

Es –
thou art a fool;

Est –
he is a crocodile sitting on a stool.

ROMAN RULERS

Julius Caesar, the Roman geezer,
Squashed his wife in a lemon squeezer.

127

Julius Caesar said with a smile
" 1760 yards in a mile. "
Said Julius Caesar before the massacre
" 4840 square yards in an acre. "

128

Julius Caesar made a law,
  Augustus Caesar signed it,
That every one that made a sneeze
  Should run away and find it.

129

Greek Alphabet

Alpha, Beta, Gamma, Delta,
   Knock the old witch down and pelt 'er.
Epsilon, Zeta, Eta, Theta,
   Pick her up again and beat 'er.

FUNNY FRENCH

130

Je suis –
I am a pot of jam;
Tu es –
thou art a fool;
Il est –
he is the biggest ass
That ever went to school.

131

Je suis –
I am a pot of jam;
Tu es –
thou art a juicy fart.

Twentieth-Century
Alphabet

A for 'orses
[hay for horses]

D for dumb
[deaf or dumb]

E for brick
[heave a brick]

G for police
[chief of police]

B for mutton
[beef or mutton]

C for yourself
[see for yourself]

F for vescence
[effervescence]

H for retirement
[age for retirement]

I for tower
[Eiffel tower]

J for oranges
[Jaffa oranges]

K for teria
[cafeteria]

N for dig
[infra dig]

O for the garden wall
[over the garden wall]

Q for a bus
[queue for a bus]

L for leather
[hell for leather]

M for sis
[emphasis]

P for comfort
[pee for comfort]

R for mo
[arf a mo]

S for you
[as for you]

T for two
[tea for two]

V for la France
[vive la France]

W for tune
[double your fortune]

Z for breezes
[zephyr breezes]

U for mism
[euphemism]

X for breakfast
[eggs for breakfast]

Y for husband
[wife or husband]

On Some Famous
Teachers

133

I do not like thee, Doctor Fell,
The reason why I cannot tell;
But this I know, and know full well,
I do not like thee, Doctor Fell.

[*Dr. John Fell, 1625–1686*
Dean of Christ Church College, Oxford]

134

Blessed be the memory
Of good old Thomas Sutton,
Who gave us lodging, learning,
As well as beef and mutton.

[Thomas Sutton, 1532–1611
Founder of Charterhouse, 1611]

135

First come I; my name is Jowett,
There is no knowledge but I know it.
I am master of this college:
What I don't know isn't knowledge.

[Benjamin Jowett, 1817–1893
Master of Balliol College, Oxford]

136

Miss Buss and Miss Beale
Cupid's darts do not feel;
How different from us
Miss Beale and Miss Buss.

[*Miss Buss, 1827–1894, Principal of*
North London Collegiate School;
Miss Beale, 1831–1906, Principal of
Ladies' College, Cheltenham]

LAMENTATION

137

Nobody loves me,
Everybody hates me,
Going in the garden
To-eat-worms.

Big fat juicy ones,
Little squiggly niggly ones.
Going in the garden
To-eat-worms.

138

Latin is a dead tongue,
Dead as dead can be.
First it killed the Romans –
Now it's killing me.

139

Multiplication is vexation,
Division is as bad,
The Rule of Three doth puzzle me,
And practice drives me mad.

140

Moods and Tenses
    Bother my senses;
Adverbs, Pronouns,
    Make me roar.
Irregular Verbs
    My sleep disturb,
They are a regular bore.

141

My head doth ache,
My hand doth shake,
    I have a naughty pen;
My ink is bad,
My pen is worse,
    How can I write well then ?

REPROACHFULNESS

142

Don't care was made to care,
Don't care was hung,
Don't care was put in a pot
And boiled till he was done.

[*Rebuke to "Don't care"*]

143

Give a thing, take it back,
Dance upon the Devil's back.

[*For one who takes back a gift*]

144

Tomorrow come never
When two Sundays come together.

[*Rebuke to a procrastinator*]

145

If "ifs" and "ans"
Were pots and pans,
There'd be no work for tinkers' hands.

[*Rebuke for too much supposition*]

SEASONAL

FEBRUARY 14TH – VALENTINE'S DAY

146

Postman, Postman, at the gate,
Will you take this to my date ?
Postman, Postman, for a laugh,
Do the tango up the path.

" Roses are red,
Violets are blue,
The shorter the skirt
The better the view.

Roses are red,
Cabbages are green,
If my face is funny,
Yours is a scream. "

April 1st – All Fools' Day

147

Fool, fool, April fool,
You learn nought by going to school.

[*Said before midday*]

148

April fool's gone past,
You're the biggest fool at last;
When April fool comes again,
You'll be the biggest fool then.

[*Said after midday*]

October 31st – Halloween

149

This is the night of Halloween
When the witches can be seen;
Some are red and some are green
And some are the color of a turkey bean.

November 5th – Guy Fawkes's Day

150

Guy, guy, guy!
Stick him up on high;
Hang him on a lamp post
And leave him there to die.

151

Please to remember
The Fifth of November,
Gunpowder treason and plot;
I know no reason
Why gunpowder treason
Should ever be forgot.
Ladies and Gentlemen you'll never grow fat,
If you don't put a penny in the old Guy's hat.

152

Knock at the knocker,
Ring at the bell,
Give us a copper
For singing so well.

153

Christmas is coming
   And the geese are getting fat,
      Please put a penny in the old man's hat,
If you haven't got a penny,
   A ha'penny will do,
      If you haven't got a ha'penny –
        God bless you !

CONTEMPT

154

Tell tale tit,
Your tongue shall be slit,
And every little dog in town
Shall have a little bit.

[*For sneaks*]

155

Cry, baby, cry,
Stick a finger in your eye,
And tell your mother it wasn't I.

[*For cry babies*]

156

Cowardy, cowardy, custard,
Can't eat bread and mustard.

[*For those who run away*]

157

Sluggardy-guise,
Loth to go to bed,
And loth to rise.

[*For the lazy*]

158

Liar, liar, lick spit,
Turn about the candlestick.
What's good for liars?
Brimstone and fires.

[*For the fibber*]

159

Trim, Tran,
Like master, like man.

[*For the copy cat*]

160

Dicky, Dicky Dout,
Your shirt's hanging out,
Four yards in, and five yards out.

[*For the badly dressed*]

INCANTATION

161

TO THE RAIN

Rain, rain, go away,
Come another summer's day;
Rain, rain, pour down,
And come no more to our town.

162

TO THE SNOW

Snow, snow faster,
The cow's in the pasture.

Snow, snow, give over,
The cow's in the clover.

163

To the Snail

Snail, snail, come out of your hole,
Or else I'll beat you as black as a coal

164

To the Ladybird

Ladybird, ladybird, fly away home.
Your house is on fire, your children all gone.

165

To the Crow

Crow, crow, get out of my sight,
Or else I'll have your liver and light.

166

To the Seagull

Seagull, seagull, sit on the sand,
It's never good weather when you're inland.

167

To the Puss Moth

Millery, millery, dustipole,
How many sacks have you stole?
Four and twenty and a peck,
Hang the miller up by his neck.

LULLABIES —
ADOLESCENT STYLE

168

Good night, sleep tight,
  Don't let the bugs bite;
If they do, don't squall,
  Take a spoon and eat them all.

169

On a still calm night when the bugs begin to bite
  And the fleas run away with the pillow,
If I had a string I would make their ears ring
  And make them come back with my pillow.

170

Good night, sweet repose;
  Half the bed and all the clothes.

171

Good night and sweet repose,
  I hope the fleas will bite your nose;
And every bug as big as a bee
  And then you'll have good company.

END OF TERM

172

Today's the case,
Tomorrow's the trunk,
Day after that
We all do a bunk.

Today's the brush,
Tomorrow's the comb,
And after that
We all go home.

Today's the saucer
Tomorrow's the cup,
If you don't give us hollies
We'll all break up.

173

This time tomorrow, where shall I be ?
Not in this academy !

No more Latin, no more French,
No more sitting on a hard school bench.

No more dirty bread and butter,
No more water from the gutter.

No more maggots in the ham,
No more yukky bread and jam.

No more milk in dirty old jugs,
   No more cabbage boiled with slugs.

No more spiders in my bath,
   Trying hard to make me laugh.

No more beetles in my tea,
   Making googly eyes at me.

No more things to bring us sorrow,
   'Cos we won't be here tomorrow.

174

F FOR FINNY

I FOR INNY

N FOR NICKLEBRANDY

I FOR ISAAC PAINTER'S WIFE

S FOR SUGAR CANDY

NOTES

*The numerals refer
to verse numbers.*

2. Sometimes they just say:

> I saw
> Esau
> Sitting on a seesaw.

3. This may have been a music hall song of the down-to-earth kind beloved by Londoners. In the late 1940s in Barnes, on the banks of the Thames, an old gentleman of seventy-four was overheard singing:

> I had a bloke, he was
>   double-jointed,
> I kissed him, made him
>   disappointed;
> First he died, then I had
>   another one,
> Gawd bless his heart, better
>   than the other one.

5. In one version mother "roasted it and toasted it" before she had it for her tea; in another "the flea died and mother cried."

8. We didn't give her a thought when we used to sing this, but we were perpetuating, probably, a lampoon against the rejected and much-taunted wife of George IV.

10. Or:

> Thomas a Didymus,
>   King of the Jews,
> Jumped into the fire
>   and burned both his shoes.

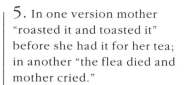

Or:

> Thomas a Didymus
>   had a black beard,
> Kiss'd Nancy Fitchett
>   and made her afear'd.

Thomas a Didymus was the apostle who doubted that Christ had risen from the dead. *Didymus* means *twin*.

Wife selling was a recognized custom as late as the beginning of the nineteenth century. If a man's wife were willing, he could take her to market with a halter around her neck and sell her to the highest bidder. It was, in fact, a poor man's form of divorce, and sometimes suited all parties. See also no. 98.

11. Peter Opie suffered from this gibe as a child.

12. This rhyme may originally have been intended to poke fun at the speech of country bumpkins. In some dialects words ending in *st* kept the ancient plural – as *nestes* and *frostes*. Often this was extended to yet another syllable, and a farm laborer might be heard saying, "They there postesses are all rotten."

13. This rhyme comes from Norman Douglas's "breathless catalogue," *London Street Games*, 1916, as do nos. 16, 36 (slightly adapted), 43, 46, 76, 78, and 97.

14. Considered to be a suitable reply to the adult admonition:

Patience is a virtue,
Virtue is a grace;
Both put together
Make a very pretty face.

15. One of the oldest forms of nonsense. About 1480 a professional minstrel jotted down in his notebook (now in the Bodleian Library, Oxford) the following amusement:

I saw iij hedles
    playen at a ball,
An hanlas man
    served hem all,
Whyll iij movthles
    men lay & low,
Iij legles a-way hem drow.

Which translates as:

I saw three headless [men]
    playing at ball,
A handless man served
    them all,
While three mouthless [men]
    sang and howled,
Three legless [men]
    drove them away.

21. These are the lines that brought us under the spell of schoolchild lore. We were leaning out of a window of our country home one evening in 1946, when a small boy went by intoning them. They seemed to us strange, primitive and utterly fascinating.

23. Said by a large boy to a smaller one to make the smaller one get out of his way.

31. Occurrences like this make the folklorist excited and the rest of us think that it is a small world. When we first found the rhyme, we believed it to be obsolete. It used to be repeated in front of Warwickshire houses having TO LET signs in the window. Then we saw an extract from an article in *The New Yorker* of November 1937, giving sidewalk rhymes of the skyscraper city. This was one of them:

Floor to let,
Inquire within;
Lady put out
For drinking gin.

If she promises to drink
  no more,
Here's the key to her
  back door.

35. Or, a Cheshire variant:

It rains, it pains,
It patters i' th' docks;
Mobberley wenches are
  washing their smocks.

39. The letter *r*.

40. Andrew. Well-known today, this was also known to a Mr. Randle Holme of Chester three hundred years ago. (MS Harley, 1960, folio 15.)

41. Or "What is black and white and re[a]d all over?"

42. Some people can never be convinced that he is looking at a portrait of his son.

43. Undoubtedly a relative of Peter, Pumpkin Eater, who:

Had a wife and couldn't
    keep her,
Had another, didn't love her,
Causing instantaneous
    bother.

44. The plot of Dorothy Sayers's story "Uncle Meleager's Will" hinges on this rhyme.

46. In the U.S.A., "Teddy on the railroad." Early versions are about "Paddy on the railway," and it is more than likely that the song once made fun of (or fun for) the Irish gangers who first built the railroads.

47. This must have been familiar to British music hall audiences. The well-known comedy team of Elsie Ravenall and Gracie West used it in their act in the 1920s and '30s.

48. Or, from Scotland:

Dicky Dan was
    a funny wee man,
He washed his head
    in a tarry pan,
He combed his hair
    with the leg of a chair,
Dicky Dan was
    a funny wee man.

Or, from the U.S.A.:

Your mother, my mother,
    live across the way;
Every night they have
    a fight,
And this is what they say:
Your old man is a dirty
    old man,
'Cos he washes his face
    in a frying pan,
He combs his hair
With the leg of the chair;
Your old man is a dirty
    old man.

49. Readers of F. Anstey's *Vice Versa* may remember this.

51. The painful custom of pinching anyone discovered wearing something new was in full force during our school life.

52. This reproof is in *The London Treasury*, 1933. We don't know how old it is, but it seems to have traveled. When an American child wants to say the same thing, he says:

"Silence in the court room! The judge wants to spit."

We imagine there were two more lines, similar to the English, which have been lost.
   The non-poetic achieve a tense hush with:

"Silence in the pig market – let the old sow speak first."

53. "Said by a youngster who takes gravel, earth, etc., and casts it into the air. Companions take warning at the first phrase, and run a short distance to escape the shower." G. F. Northall, *English Folk-Rhymes*, 1892.

54. Joseph Ritson included the challenge in *Gammer Gurton's Garland*, 1784. "Here stands a post" is perhaps a better-known first line. The British music hall singer known as The Great Macdermott (holding a Union Jack) used to sing a patriotic song, "Here Stands a Post," which was undoubtedly based on the rhyme. It was addressed to the Russians at the time Constantinople was threatened.

55. Chambers, in *Popular Rhymes of Scotland*, 1842, says that it was the custom for bands of youths to parade the streets at night shouting such a rhyme as this "at the full extent of their voices." The words were written down a hundred years earlier in *Tommy Thumb's Pretty Song Book*, c. 1744.

56. To find out whether it is time for class to be dismissed, the pupil holds a book between his knees and measures along its length with his two forefingers, one after the other. The last finger having enough space to rest on the book provides the answer.

57. One of the many parodies of Felicia Hemans's poem "Casabianca," which begins, "The boy stood on the burning deck."

61. "Hi-tiddley-i-ti!" was a popular exclamation, in vogue c. 1890, which grew into the rhythmic catch phrase "Hi-tiddley-i-ti, brown bread!" (in the U.S.A., "Shave and a hair-cut, bay rum!"); and that, in turn, spawned various folk rhymes. The text verse was the best known of these. Another ran:

Hi-tiddley-i-ti, brown bread;
Look at your father's –
    bald head!

62. Sent to us by an 11-year-old girl from Hackney, London in 1952. It goes to the marching tune of "The Girl I Left Behind Me," and is the kind of joyful song to sing when walking home from school.

64. "Said to small folk to chaff them." G. F. Northall, *English Folk-Rhymes*, 1892.

66. Number 106 is another of these curious rhymes. The device seems to be for the aid of the tormented – a substitute for sharp-wittedness. It does not matter exactly what the reply is as long as it is prompt. "What's your name? What's your name? What's your name?" The ridiculous, oft-repeated inquiry by people who no doubt know the answer perfectly well is shown up by an equally ridiculous response.

The version we give was
used by schoolboys at
Eton College c. 1830.
Another which used
to echo in Eton's
cloisters was:

Who's your tutor,
Who's your dame,
What's your form,
And what's your name?

67. This rebuke for those
who dislike what is fair was
described by J. O. Halliwell in
Popular Rhymes, 1849, as "still
a universal favourite with
children." Twelve years later
a correspondent to *Notes and
Queries* was asking, "What has
become of the rest of 'tit for
tat'? ... I can find nobody
nowadays who remembers
having heard the whole." Two
decades later, in 1883, W. W.
Newell told how the same
words were being used for a
game of chance by American
children.

68. This is the most telling
kind of insult, which begins
with deceptive politeness.
Another such is:

If I do live till Easter Day,
And God do give me grace,
I'll give thee a bowl of water
To wash thy dirty face.

69. This is the reply when
anyone complains of being
stared at. The first line, at least,
has been common for centuries.
It appeared in John Heywood's
proverb *Dialogue*, 1546: "What,
a cat maie looke on a King, ye
know."

70–74. The counting-out
samples included here are
spiced with juvenile
improvisations (and were thus
eligible for this collection).
They bear but few traces of
the pre-Roman Anglo-Cymric

numerals from which they spring. In the nursery, however, passed on by faithful grandmas and grandpas, there are still to be heard selection formulas in a fair state of preservation.

75 & 77–80. Rhymes repeated while skipping. In no. 75 the tempo increases as the rhyme ends, so that at the word *pepper,* those who hold the rope whirl it around as fast as the skipper can skip – or faster.

Nos. 77 and 80 are for finding out something – the number of funeral coaches or the initial of a sweetheart. Each jump has a number or a letter: when the rope gets tangled in the legs, it gives the answer. No. 79 is still one of the most popular skipping rhymes, because of the tricky actions that must be done:

on the last line the skipper puts one foot on each side of the rope.

Little girls always enjoy skipping to lugubrious songs about death. The forerunner of no. 78 is the chorus of the Jacobite song that was sung to Boswell and Dr. Johnson by their host on the Isle of Skye in 1773 "when he was merry over a glass":

Green sleeves and
    pudding pies,
Tell me where
    my mistress lies,
And I'll be with her
    before she rise,
Fiddle and a' together.

81. Chant for ending a person's turn on a swing. After the two big pushes that throw the swinger "over the garden wall," no more pushes are given and the swing is allowed to die down.

83. An amalgam of two versions of a chant of dark religious resonance, which was used by heedless little girls for bouncing a ball against a wall

in Morpeth, Northumberland, c. 1890, and Sunderland, Durham, c. 1940. The first two lines contain the folk names for the Sundays in Lent and Easter Day itself. The last line reveals that the real use of the rhyme is for hopscotch, called pot or potsy in the north east of England; the pot was a semi-circular space at the top of the diagram, which, as well as being Home, was used as a receptacle for the score.

84. The many variations extend from the sacred to the frivolous and to the downright unprintable.

Matthew, Mark, Luke and John,
Went to bed with their
trousers on...

and:

Matthew, Mark, Luke and John,
Get a stick and lay it hard on ...

are simply deviations from the rhyming evening prayer that starts:

Matthew, Mark, Luke and John,
Bless the bed that I lie on.

85. Remembered by P. H. Gosse from his Dorsetshire school days, c. 1820.

86. "Well known as a schoolboy's catch for the innocent new boy and for our unwary sisters when I was at school fifty years ago," said a writer in *Notes and Queries*, 1906. An older version is:

James and John
And Little Nip on
Went down to the sea and
    bathed;
James and John
They tumbled in,
Now guess you who was saved.

The question is still popular with the questioners among schoolchildren today.

87. Well over a hundred years old (J. O. Halliwell recorded it in 1844), it is still tried out by

the ever-hopeful young of
both England and America.
Similar is:

I am a gold lock,
I am a gold key.
I am a silver lock,
I am a silver key.
I am a brass lock,
I am a brass key.
I am a monk (or don) lock,
I am a monk (or don) key.

88. Another recalled by Mr
Gosse. "The stranger came in
due course to 'I'll go to L,' when
a cry of affected surprise is
raised: 'Lo! what d'ye think? He
says he'll go to hell!'" It is
an alarming thought that
these same tricks have been
set to catch new boys for the
past hundred and seventy
years or so.

89. The earliest puzzle we
had to cope with. We
remembered, when seven or
eight years old, repeating and
repeating the lines to
ourselves and not making
sense of them – not for several
months! We were delighted

to find them appearing in
*A Choice Collection of Riddles,
Charades, Rebusses, etc.*, by
Peter Puzzlewell, Esq., 1792.
The correct punctuation, of
course, is:

Charles the First walked and
    talked;
Half an hour after, his head
    was cut off.

90. Punctuated correctly,
reads:

Every lady in the land
Has twenty nails: upon each
    hand
Five, and twenty on hands
    and feet;
All this is true without deceit.

91. In plain English:

In fir tar is,
In oak none is.
In mud eels are,
In clay none are.
Mares eat oats,
Goats eat ivy.

The last two lines were given
notoriety as the basis of the
lyric "Mairzy Doats," a swing

song contagious in America and Britain in the summer of 1943. With a touching naivety, the words were claimed as original. In a volume of medical collectanea of the fifteenth century by William Wyrcestre is recorded:

Is thy pott enty, Colelent?
Is gote eate yvy.
Mare eate ootys.
Is thy cocke lyke owrs?

92. A style of quip popular in the seventeenth century. It was repeated by George Herbert in *Witts Recreations*, 1641; by the Reverend and learned John Ray, F. R. S., in 1678; and by that celebrated American, Benjamin Franklin, in 1746. Subsequently echoed by hundreds of a more tender age – less learned and less celebrated, but possibly more in earnest about the sentiment of the rhyme.

95. The response when accused of being standoffish.

96. One of the many rhymes for teasing those named Charlie; this one came from Maryland, 1947. "Why," said a correspondent to *Notes and Queries*, 1902, whose initials were C. C. B., "should this name be so distinguished above others?"

98. When P.H. Gosse was at school, in about 1820, he used to repeat:

My needle and thread
Spells Nebuchadned;
My bodkin and scissors
Spells Nebuchadnezzar;
One pair of stockings and
    two pair of shoes
Spells Nebuchadnezzar the
    King of the Jews.

101. Collected by G. F. Northall in Warwickshire, *English Folk-Rhymes*, 1892. He said it was "sometimes used as a street shout to any obnoxious Mary."

103. In the hope that a rude word may seem to be said.

104. "I will, THAT" as the compiler (possibly Oliver Goldsmith) added to the rhyme when he included it in *Mother Goose's Melody*, about 1765. There are numerous variations, as:

Spell me that without a P,
And a clever scholar you
    will be.

105. CO-CO-A.

106. Or:

What do they call you?
Patchy Dolly.
Where were you born?
In the cow's horn.
Where were you bred?
In the cow's head.
Where will you die?
In the cow's eye.

Or:

What's your name?
Baldy Bane.
What's your other?
Ask my mother.
Where do you sleep?
Among the sheep.
Where do you lie?
Among the kye [cows].
Where do you take your
    brose [oatmeal stirabout]?
Up and down the cuddy's
    [donkey's] nose.

107. Yes, T-H-A-T.

109–113. For some reason, as one knows to one's cost, *other* people's moral scruples desert them when it comes to book borrowing. "Although most of my friends are bad arithmeticians, they are all good book-keepers," as Sir Walter Scott put it. And apparently it always has been so. In 1578 F. Camerarii found it necessary to inscribe in his Aristotle:

This boke is one thing,
The halter is another
And he that stealeth the one,
Must be sure of the other.

114. *Aren't some people inquisitive!*

115. A trick!

119 & 120. Jingles similar to "Infir taris" (no. 91). The "translations" are:

Brutus 'ad some jam for tea,
Caesar 'ad a rat.
Brutus sick in omnibus,
Caesar sick in 'at.

I say, Billy, here's a go,
Forty buses in a row.
No, Billy, them is trucks,
See vot is in 'em – peas
   an' ducks.

121–123. Variations on a theme. The first two were collected in the late nineteenth century. No. 123 is from c. 1945. In a play, *The Agreeable Surprise*, 1782, appears:

Amo, amas,
I love a lass,
She is so sweet and tender;
It is sweet cowslips grace
In the nominative case
And in the feminine gender.

126–128. Making fun of Julius Caesar was the schoolboy's way of getting his own back for tedious hours spent with the Gallic Wars. Augustus Caesar is here as a supernumerary only.

129. A version of the rhyme remembered from his school days and used for the entertainment of his students by Professor Gilbert Murray, Regius Professor of Greek at Oxford University from 1908 to 1936.

133. The story is that Dr. Fell was about to expel the satirist Tom Brown (1663-1704) but said the sentence would be remitted if Tom could translate extempore the lines from Martial:

Non amo te, Sabidi, nec
  possum dicere quare;
Hoc tantum possum dicere,
  Non amo te.

Tom Brown's immediate rendering was the epigram now well known. He is said to have been allowed to stay on at the college and, incidentally, by 1686 had sufficiently overcome his dislike of the doctor to write him a complimentary epitaph.

The doctor of divinity and the satirist alike would have relished Maurice Sendak's further translation of the rhyme into schoolchild literality.

134. Thomas Sutton was the owner of coal mines in Durham and one of the richest men of his time. In the year of his death he founded a charity school at Hallingbury Bouchers, Essex, "for the education and maintenance of forty boys"; its successor is the famous Charterhouse public school of the present day, at Godalming, Surrey.

136. Frances Buss and Dorothea Beale were the principals of the first two British public schools for girls, the North London Collegiate and Cheltenham Ladies' College. The girls may well have thought them austere, for these great pioneers were determined that their pupils should achieve the same educational standards as their brothers and required of them an absolute devotion to learning.

139. This commonly heard lament has made the journey from Queen Elizabeth's reign. In a manuscript dated 1570 it reads:

Multiplication is mie
    vexation
And division quite as bad,
The Golden rule is mie
    stumbling stule,
And Practice makes me mad.

"The Rule of Three," or
"Golden Rule," was a way of
finding a fourth number from
three given numbers, by using
proportions. "Practice" was the
finding of the value of so many
articles at so many pounds,
shillings, and pence each.

143. There is no crime more
heinous among school
children than wanting a
possession back once it has
been given. Plato says the
same sentiment was
proverbial with the children
of his day. Other versions
have been,

1611:

To give a thing and take
    a thing;
To wear the divell's gold ring.

1678:

Give a thing and take again,
And you shall ride in hell's
    wain.

Scottish, 1842:

Gi'e a thing, tak' a thing,
Auld man's gowd ring;
Lie butt, lie ben,
Lie among the deid men.

146. Verses such as these,
written on scraps of paper and
ornamented with bleeding
hearts, are passed across the
classrooms of Britain and
America on St. Valentine's Day.

147 & 148. On the first of
April "you may send a fool
wherever you will." But not
after 12 o'clock, or you become
more fool yourself than the

fool you were hoping to make. In Scotland a yet greater April noddy, noodle, lown, or gowk is he who attempts to make a fool on April 2nd, and such an attempt can be withered by:

April-day is come and gone,
Thou art a gosling and I am
  none.

The Feast of Folly is observed in practically every land. Nobody knows for certain of what it is in honor. Tradition, which paints as pretty a picture as any, says that April 1st was the day when Noah first sent the dove from the Ark and the search for land was fruitless.

149. Halloween, the eve of the Celtic New Year, was a time when evil spirits were at large. Children (and, indeed, grown-ups) still commemorate this spooky night by dressing up as witches and ghosts. It is an old custom in Scotland and the far north of England for children, in disguise, to go around their neighborhood asking for small

gifts and threatening to play tricks on householders who give them nothing. This custom has now invaded the south of England from America, where it is widespread under the name of Trick or Treat.

150 & 151. There is plenty of evidence to show that Britain has celebrated November 5th with bonfires and Guy-burning continuously since 1606. (The Guy Fawkes bonfires, incidentally, replaced the earlier tradition of bonfires on All Saints' Eve.) A historical occasion when the custom proved useful was in 1688, when William of Orange's arrival in England was delayed until the Fifth so that he might think that the people were feting him.

The versions we give are, of course, still often repeated. At Lewes, where Gunpowder Plot Day receives the attention it deserves, various societies exist to carry on the celebrations. One of their rhymes, printed here on the authority of the Public Librarian of Lewes, in Sussex, is:

Please to remember the Fifth
  of November,
Gunpowder treason and plot;
I see no reason why
  Gunpowder treason
Should ever be forgot.
Guy Fawkes, Guy,
  'twas his intent
To blow up the King
  and the Parliament;
Three score barrels laid below
To prove old England's
  overthrow.
By God's providence
  he was catch'd
With a dark lantern
  and lighted match.
Holloa, boys,
    holloa, boys,
      make the
        bells ring,

Holloa, boys, holloa, boys,
  God save the King!
A farthing loaf
  to feed old Pope,
A penn'orth of cheese
  to choke him,
A pint of beer
  to rinse it down,
And a faggot of wood
  to burn him!
Burn him in a tub of tar,
Burn him like a blazing star,
Burn his body from his head,
Then we'll say old Pope
  is dead!
Hip, hip, hoo-r-r-ray!

The pope, it may be added, is represented by a pole in the center of the fire. And, incidentally, this is the best way to make a bonfire, with a strong upright in the middle.

154. An early version is in *Tommy Thumb's Pretty Song Book*, c. 1744:

Spit Cat, Spit,
Your tongue shall be slit,
And all the Dogs
In our Town,
Shall have a bit.

158. The expression in the first line is very old; see *Gammer Gurton's Needle*, 1575. The whole rhyme is referred to in Henry Carey's ballad "Namby Pamby," c. 1720:

Now he sings of
   'Lick-spit Liar
Burning in the
   Brimstone Fire;
Lyar, Lyar, Lick-spit, lick,
Turn about the
   Candle-stick.'

J. O. Halliwell, in *Popular Rhymes*, 1849, gives the following lines as the schoolboys' condemnation of a liar in his day:

Liar, liar, lick dish,
Turn about the candlestick.

159. *The Oxford English Dictionary* traces this taunt from 1583 ("Trim tram, neither good for God nor man"), through Smollett, 1762, to T. Gibson, 1877 ("Trin tran, sike like master sike like man / A lazy life brings scant or scan"). It is probably obsolete now except in dialect.

161–167. Incantations come under the heading of folk rhymes. Those here, however, are mostly repeated by children.

161. Some well-known variations are:

Raine, raine, goe away,
Come againe a Saturday.

believed to be of great antiquity by John Aubrey, writing in 1687.

Raine, raine, goe to Spain,
Faire weather come againe.

first recorded in James Howell's *Proverbs*, 1659.

Rain, rain, go away,
Come again April day,
Little Johnny wants to play.

recorded in 1805.

163. This is an example of the same rhyme and rite being repeated by children in almost all European languages and, we are told, some Asiatic ones, too. As well as from different parts of Britain, we have gathered versions from Russia,

France, Naples, Tuscany, Silesia, and Spain. Nobody knows the origin and significance of this address to the snail.

164. The same applies to this rhyme, and the rite which attends it, as to the last one. It is familiar in many countries. The ladybird (*Coccinella septempunctata* or *Coccinella bipunctata*), also called the ladyfly, ladybug, ladycow, Judy-cow, dowdy-cow, God's little cow, Lady Landers, cusha-coo-lady, Marygold, May-bug, golden bug, burnie-bee, Bishop Barnabee, and King Galloway, according to where you live, is usually considered to augur good fortune. The well-known version we have chosen comes from *Tommy Thumb's Pretty Song Book*, c. 1744.

165. A crow can be unlucky. The need for this rhyme, which country children commonly address to the bird, lies in the superstition that a solitary crow flying across one's path augurs bad fortune.

167. Address to the puss moth, the dusty white male of which looks as if it has been pilfering flour. The expression "Now, miller, miller, dustipole" is used by Robin Goodfellow in the play *Grim, the Collier of Croydon*, c. 1600. J. O. Halliwell recorded and described the rhyme in 1849, and, in *Country Life*, 1941, Llewelyn Powys told of the same rhyme and practice being current.

169. Calculated, no doubt, to make one "snug as a bug in a rug."

173. Rarely is so much enthusiasm displayed during our lives as for the approaching end of term at school, heralded by this prince of rhymes. We have no ideas about its age; some of the lines were given to us by a lady of ninety in 1946. American children have their own variations; for instance, in Maryland, 1947:

No more pencils,
　　no more books,
No more teacher's
　　sassy looks.

174. FINIS, FINJS, FJNIS and FJNJS. Some of these variations must be old from the way they ignore the difference between I and J.

F for Finis
I for Inis
N for Nuckley Bone,
I for John the Waterman
S for Samuel Stone.

And:

F for Flo and J for Joe
And N for Naughty Nellie,
I for Ire from temper's fire,
And S for Stink and Smelly.

And:

F for France, and J for Jance,
And N for Nickley Boney,
J for John the 'prentice boy,
And S for Sammy Coney.

And:

F is for Fanny, and I is for
    Jane,
N is for Nanny who lives up
    the lane,
I is for ink and S is for stink
FINIS to you I now explain.

PENG.